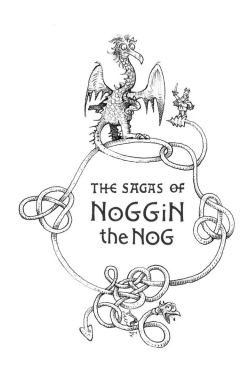

THE SAGAS of
NoGGiN
the NoG

Formerly published as The Saga of Noggin the Nog by Collins 1992
This edition published by The Dragons' Friendly Society, 2007

Text © Oliver Postgate 1968
Illustrations © Peter Firmin 1992
Printed and bound in the UK

ISBN 978-1-903708-24-8

The Dragons' Friendly Society
Liverpool L18 9UR

www.dragonsfriendly.co.uk

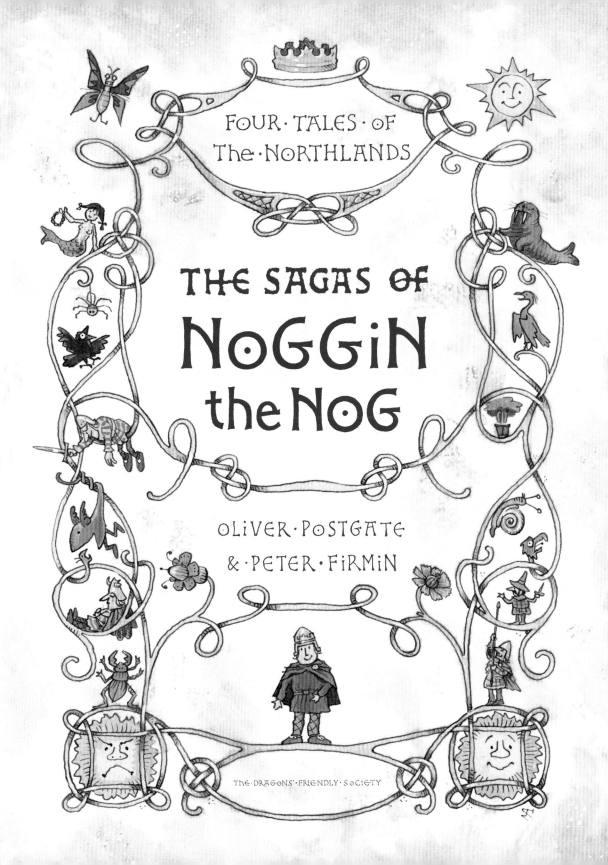

FOUR · TALES · OF
THE · NORTHLANDS

THE SAGAS OF
NOGGIN
the NOG

OLIVER · POSTGATE
& · PETER · FIRMIN

THE · DRAGONS' · FRIENDLY · SOCIETY

CONTENTS

1

KiNG
of the
NOGS

N THE LANDS OF THE NORTH, WHERE THE BLACK
rocks stand guard against the cold sea, in the dark
night that is very long, the Men of the Northlands
sit by their great log fires and they tell a tale.

They tell of a prince and how he built a long ship and sailed beyond
the black ice at the edge of the world to bring home his bride from the
land of the Midnight Sun.

Noggin the Nog was the name of the prince. He was the son of Knut,
King of the Nogs, the aged ruler of that land of dark forest and snow
which men call the land of Nog.

Now, every morning King Knut would rise from his bed, put on his
boots and climb to the hill above the royal castle. At the top of this hill
was a rock known as Knut's seat. The aged king would sit on the seat
and as the sun rose behind the mountains he would begin to worry.

He would look down on the little town clustered around the castle walls and he would worry about his people and whether their roofs leaked and whether they had warm socks this cold weather. He would look down on his castle and he would worry about his son, Prince Noggin, and what would happen to his people if Noggin did not marry soon; for it is the law in the Northland that the king shall be married. The old king knew that if he died Noggin would have to marry within six weeks of his death or he would not become king, and then the crown would go to his wicked uncle, Nogbad the Bad.

The people of the town would look up at their king sitting there worrying and they would say: "Don't worry old king," but of course the king would go on worrying just the same.

Then, one day, the king rose from his seat as if to go down to his castle. The people watching him saw him shake and stagger and fall to the ground. The king was dead. Great was the sadness and loud the wailing. The flags on the houses were pulled to half mast and the great bell rang. All were sad, save one. In his black castle Nogbad the Bad heard the distant sounds of sorrow and smiled a greedy smile.

In the Royal Castle, Noggin's mother, Queen Grunhilda rose from her bed and called for the prince.

"Noggin," she said, "the time has come for you to choose a bride. I shall summon all the maidens of gentle birth to the castle within seven days, and on the seventh day you shall choose your bride."

Soon the sound of trumpets was heard throughout the land as, from the battlements of the castles, from the balconies of the tallest houses the royal heralds proclaimed their message.

What excitement there was among the maidens! What twittering and giggling! With hopeful hearts they put on their walking shoes and skipped away to the Royal Castle.

On the seventh day the maidens assembled, dozens of them, in lines across the hall. Slowly Noggin the Nog walked along the lines looking with great care and friendliness. There were tall girls, short girls, lean girls from the valleys with hair as black as ravens' wings, fat girls from the castles on the mountain top with golden plaits and eyes as blue as the sky.

Noggin came to the end of the line and he had not chosen. He had not found one maiden that pleased him enough to make her his queen.

Standing calmly next to the very last maiden of all, Noggin saw a large green bird, a strange bird, the like of which he had never seen before.

"You are not a maiden, you are a bird," he said.

"Your highness is observant," said the bird. "My name is Graculus. I have flown from the land of the Midnight Sun and from my master, Nan of the Nooks, I bring you greetings and a gift." The bird took from under his wing a knife. He placed it in Noggin's hand.

"Thank you very much," said Noggin. He looked at the knife. It was made from a single faultless walrus tooth. On it was carved the likeness of a girl's face. Noggin looked at the face and he thought it beautiful, more beautiful than any of the maidens he had seen that day, or any other day for that matter.

"Who is this maiden?" he asked.

"It is the likeness of my master's daughter," said the bird. "It is the face of Nooka, Princess of the Nooks."

Noggin, Prince of the Nogs, turned to his people and, holding up the knife, he cried out: "This is the maiden I shall marry."

What alarm and surprise there was in the castle!

What grumbling and grumping!

With heavy hearts the maidens put on their walking shoes and trudged back to their homes.

Noggin climbed the steps in the castle yard and addressed the Royal Guard and the people of the town.

"Who will come with me?" he asked.

"We will!" cried the warriors with one voice.

"Who will build me a ship?" he asked.

"We will!" called the carpenters.

"And we will paint it!" called the painters.

"And we will make you sails!" called the sailmakers.

And so it was. The Nogs built a long ship of oak from the valleys. The mast was a single perfect pine tree. The high prow was carved and painted and gilded to a ferocious dragon's head. The sail was a square of stout canvas embroidered with the crest of Noggin and the face of Nooka. To protect the sides of the ship were shields of hammered bronze.

"Do not grieve for me, Mother," said Noggin the Nog as he took leave of Queen Grunhilda. "The ship is strong, the men are brave. Graculus will guide us through the perils of the deep."

So the ship was launched. Noggin and his band of warriors raised the great square sail with the crest of Noggin and the face of Nooka. The wind took the sail and the ship moved away down the fjord towards the sea.

The people watched from the quay and waved goodbye. Everybody was sad to see them go and afraid for their safety on the long and perilous journey. Everybody save one.

In his black castle on the hill, Nogbad the Bad looked down on the little ship and he smiled. He knew that the journey to the land of the Midnight Sun was so long and dangerous that there was little chance of Noggin coming back and, as he thought of the royal treasure, the taxes and jewels and the crown which would soon be his, he chuckled to himself.

"Huh. Huh. Huh!"

A good wind blew the ship away from the land of Nog. Night came. The helmsman lashed the steering oar to hold the helm to the North Star and the band of Nogs sat round their stove in the canvas cabin and made hot buttered toast.

All the next day and night the wind blew them on. Then, one day, the wind dropped. The sun came out and it was really quite warm. As the sun set that night a storm blew up. The wind howled in the rigging. The thunder roared, the lightning flashed as the great waves tossed the little ship about like a cork.

Graculus lay under a shelf feeling very, very sick. The Nogs huddled around their stove and prayed that the ship would not sink.

Morning came. The storm blew past and all was calm. They hoisted the sail and looked at it. No wind came to fill it. It hung limp on the mast and the ship stayed where it was, still in a calm still sea.

The Captain of the Guard, the fierce Thor Nogson, stood at the helm.

"What do we do now, Noggin?"

"Row, I suppose," replied the prince.

The oarsmen took up their oars.

"Which way do we row?" asked Thor Nogson.

"Oh dear, I don't know," said Noggin the Nog.

They could not ask Graculus; he was too seasick to talk. So the Nogs got out their fishing rods and sat in the sun and fished. They did not catch anything but it passed the time.

"Land Ho!" came a shout from the look-out.

Not much land indeed, just a small, brownish grey island in the sea.

"Row that way," said Noggin.

They rowed over to the island and Thor Nogson swung out on a rope and landed on it.

"Ooh, it's all soft and squodgy," he said, "and it's covered with sort of brown grass stuff."

"Explore the island," said Noggin.

"Explore it? I can see all of it from where I am standing! There is nothing here except this brown grass stuff."

"Dig some up," said Noggin.

They threw Thor Nogson a spade. He put it to the ground and dug.

The whole island rocked under him. It reeled and shook and one end of it rose in a hill letting out a great roar of pain.

"Earthquake!" shouted Thor Nogson.

The hill turned on them and it was a great head with fierce whiskers and long sharp teeth.

"I say, do you mind?" it said. "That hurt!"

It was a gigantic walrus. Noggin knew there was only one walrus in the world as big as that. They had met Arup, King of the Walruses.

They greeted each other as kings do and Noggin offered his guest refreshment - "A ship's biscuit perhaps?"

"A ship's biscuit?" said the Walrus. "Why, yes, that would be nice. I'm feeling a bit peckish."

Noggin's men went below and brought up a chest of biscuits.

"How would you like them?" asked Noggin.

"Oh, just throw them in, throw them in!" replied the King of the Walruses and he opened his mouth.

The Nogs picked up ship's biscuits and threw them into the great mouth until the chest was empty. Then the Walrus closed his mouth and chewed.

"Mm, delicious, haven't had ship's biscuit for years!"

"Hi, what about me?" shouted Thor Nogson.

"Throw him a biscuit somebody," said Noggin.

"No! I want to come back! You can't leave me on this monster all day!"

"Manners, Thor Nogson, manners!" said Noggin severely. "Wait till the King of the Walruses has finished his elevenses."

The walrus chewed another box of ship's biscuits with great pleasure and then offered to help them on their way.

"I am going towards the land of the Midnight Sun. If you just throw your gardener here a rope, I will give you a tow."

They threw Thor Nogson a rope. He tied it around the walrus's neck and quickly climbed back on board.

"Right away!" called Noggin. The walrus moved away though the calm water pulling the ship behind him.

Swiftly he swam. All that day and night he swam. Through the next day and night he pulled the little ship until they were past the black ice at the edge of the world. Then he stopped.

"I'll be off now," he said. "I go South here, but there is a good wind. Keep the Midday Sun behind you. Watch out for icebergs. Good luck!"

The King of the Walruses sank beneath the waves.

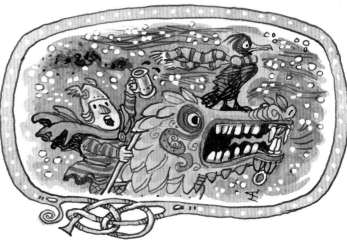

The wind bore them on. That night the snow began to fall. Graculus climbed on to the prow of the ship and guided them past the icebergs while the Nogs took turns bringing him mugs of cocoa. Then, as dawn came, they saw before them the land of the Midnight Sun. It was a flat land. No mountains and forests like their own homeland, just flat ice and snow.

Nan of the Nooks was waiting for them on the shore. He was a little man in a fur hood sitting on a throne made of blocks of ice. He was surrounded by other little men in fur hoods all jumping about with excitement.

"Greetings, Noggin the Nog. Do you come in peace?" he called.

"Hail, Nan of the Nooks. We come in peace," called Noggin the Nog as he leapt ashore.

Nan of the Nooks came down from his throne of ice and shook Noggin by the hand. "Perishing cold isn't it?" he said. "Come up to my place and have a cup of something hot."

Nan of the Nooks led Noggin to one of the round ice houses and went indoors. There was no door, only a sort of arched tunnel to crawl through. Inside, the house was bright and warm with a skin on the floor for a carpet. Nan and Noggin sat on stools and Nan's daughter brought them black tea in silver mugs.

She was Nooka, the girl whose likeness was carved on the bone knife. Noggin looked at her and she was more beautiful than he had expected.

Noggin turned to her father. He said, "Nan of the Nooks, I have come far, through hail and wind, through snowstorm and sea mist, past the black ice at the edge of the world to ask your daughter to marry me."

"Yes, I know," said Nan of the Nooks.

"Well, er …" Noggin faltered, "now I'm here, I feel a bit shy. Would you ask her for me?"

Nan of the Nooks laughed. "All right then." He called his daughter. "Nooka," he said. "Noggin has come through hail and wind through snowstorm and sea mist, past the black ice at the edge of the world to ask you to marry him. Will you marry him and be Queen of the Nogs?"

"Yes Father, I will."

So Noggin and Nooka were married. There was great feasting and merriment in the land of the Midnight Sun. Fireworks lit up the sky and the Nogs and the Nooks sang drinking songs and ate roasted caribou meat.

The next morning Graculus came to Noggin and Nooka and told them he was going to fly back to the land of Nog and tell the news that Noggin was married and on his way home. Otherwise Nogbad the Bad was sure to try and seize the throne. So Graculus flew away from the land of the Midnight Sun. Noggin, Nan and Nooka stood and waved until his strong green wings had carried him out of sight.

Far away, in the land of Nog, Nogbad the Bad stood in his black castle and looked out across the sea.

High in the air he saw a bird, a green bird, flying very slowly like a bird that is very tired. He watched the bird flutter down and with the last of its strength land on top of the flag pole, fold its wings, tuck away its head and go to sleep.

Nogbad held the flag-rope and told his guards to haul down the flag.

The guards pulled down the flag and, as they did so, Nogbad was pulled up the other side of the pole.

He reached the top and grabbed the bird by the throat.

"Aaark!" cried Graculus.

"Lower away, guards," said Nogbad.

They lowered him. He held out the bird to the guards. He said, "Take this and put it in the dungeon."

The guards took Graculus and put him in a dungeon. He sat there with a bowl of water and a bowl of birdseed and he wept. The days passed. Then one day the door was thrown open and there stood Nogbad in purple robes carrying a golden crown.

"Look at me, Bird," he said. "It is six weeks since Noggin went away. He has not returned and so, today, I go down to the council of elders in the town and they have to proclaim me King!"

Graculus watched from the barred window of the dungeon. He saw Nogbad set out in a golden carriage.

A robin perched on the window sill.

"Robin," said Graculus. "Do you want Nogbad to be king?"

The robin shook his head.

"Take this feather," said Graculus. "Put it in the hand of Queen Grunhilda and tell her I am here."

Down in the town, Nogbad the Bad drove in state past the crowds of silent people. Nobody cheered or smiled but Nogbad did not care. He thought of the royal treasure and the taxes and he smiled to himself.

In the royal castle, Queen Grunhilda stood alone by her window and looked out across the cold sea.

"Alas, my poor Noggin!" she sighed and stretched out her hand towards the horizon.

A robin landed on her hand. It was carrying a green feather.

"This is one of Graculus's feathers," said the old queen. "Where is he?"

The robin pointed with its wing towards Nogbad's castle.

The queen wasted no time. She called the guards.

"Take horses and go to the castle of Nogbad the Bad. Graculus is imprisoned there. This bird will show you the place. I am going down to the council of elders to deal with Nogbad."

At the council of elders, Nogbad was explaining what a good king he was going to be and how many extra taxes everybody would pay.

Queen Grunhilda entered the hall, "Nogbad!" she cried in ringing tones. "What is the penalty for obstructing the king's messenger?"

"The penalty is banishment, Grunhilda."

"Nogbad," she commanded, "go and pack your bags!"

The elders laughed, but Nogbad twirled his moustache and scowled.

"Madam," he began. "I could have you thrown into the dungeons for insolence, but as you were once Queen of the Nogs I will be merciful. I will let you go back to your castle, but you must stay there and mind your own business, for I am the king."

"Oh no you are not," came a voice from the doorway. There was Graculus perched on the shoulder of the captain of the Queen's Guard.

"Slink away Nogbad, your time is up!" and Nogbad slunk away.

"Smoke!" cried the boy who sold winkles.

"Smoke!" cried the harbour master.

The signal fire on the headland was burning to show that a sail had been sighted.

They saw a ship. It was tiny and far away, but Grunhilda, looking through the harbour master's telescope, could make out the crest of Nog and the face of Nooka embroidered on the sail.

Soon the ship sailed up the fjord to the harbour, where, amid great rejoicing, Noggin and Nooka stepped ashore to be greeted by their people.

Graculus told Noggin of Nogbad's wickedness and he sent soldiers to seek him out. They did not find him. Nogbad had put on his climbing boots and set off over the pass to stay with his granny in Finland.

So Noggin and Nooka came home to their kingdom.

They were crowned that day in the royal castle, Noggin and Nooka, King and Queen of the Nogs, and their reign was long and happy.

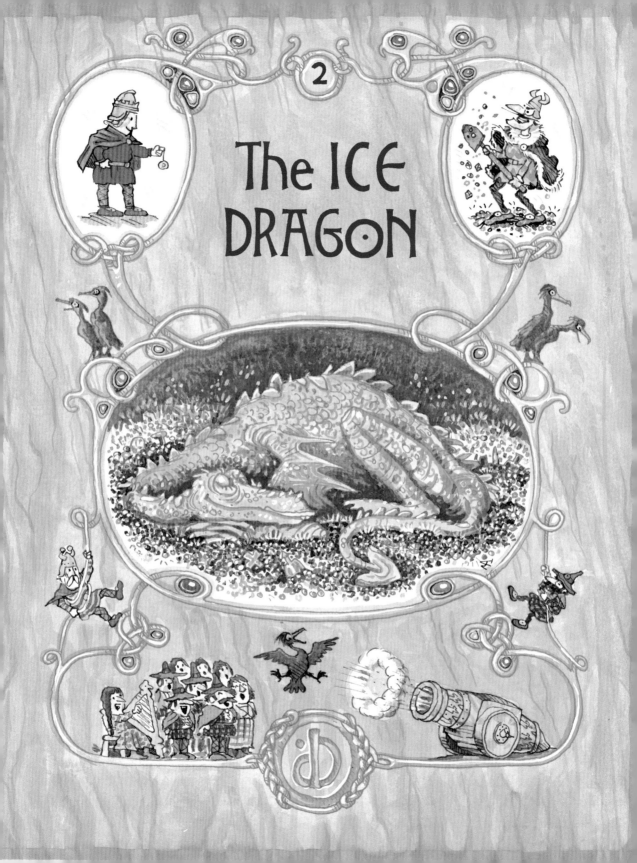

IN THE LANDS OF THE NORTH, WHERE THE BLACK rocks stand guard against the cold sea, in the dark night that is very long, the men of the Northlands sit by their great log fires and they tell a tale. They tell of a king who left his castle and his peaceful land to travel through the dark wood of Troldeskow to meet a dragon in the Hot-water Valley beyond the Glass Mountains. Noggin the Nog was the name of the king. His Queen was Nooka, the fair daughter of Nan of the Nooks.

Together they ruled over the town, the valleys, the mountains, the caves and the forests that are called the Land of Nog. Their friend and counsellor was Graculus, the great green bird who had guided Noggin to Nooka's home, the Land of the Midnight Sun.

One cold bright spring morning Graculus was flying above the castle and the town. He saw in the distance a hawk turn and drop like a winged stone into a high cleft in the mountains. He pitied the poor rabbit or hare that the hawk had chosen for its prey. Then Graculus heard a squawk, a grunt and a shout and the hawk shot out again shedding chopped feathers behind it.

"That is no rabbit," though Graculus and he glided down into the place. A sword struck sparks from the rock before him.

"Oot o' my way ye scraggy parrot!" The sword flashed again. Graculus swerved in the air. He caught a glimpse of a tiny, furious bearded face behind the sword.

"Oot o' my way ye green-faced chicken. I'll have ye for mincemeat!"

Graculus gripped a ledge of rock and perched out of reach. He spoke sternly. "If you don't stop waving that carving knife I shall drop a rock on you."

The little man lowered his sword.

"Are ye not come to eat me?" he asked.

"Indeed I am not," said Graculus, who was particular about what he ate. The man sat down and mopped his brow.

"That's a relief then. Yon hawk near had me on the hill there!"

Graculus, seeing that the sword was laid aside, came closer.

"Where are you from, little man?" he asked.

"I am from the Hot-water Valley beyond the Glass Mountains, and I am not a little man. I am the biggest and strongest in the valley."

"From the Hot-water Valley are you? I have heard that some people live there, but I had no idea they were so little."

"Well I am one of them. We are a strong people, tall as the summer grass. I'll not have ye call us little!"

The man's hand was on his sword.

Graculus backed away.

"I beg your pardon," he said. "My name is Graculus. I am the Royal Bird of the Land of Nog."

"My name is Ronf and it is to Noggin the Nog I come with a message from my people."

"Greetings, little man, and welcome to the Land of Nog."

The little man rose and put his face close to Graculus's beak.

"Greetings, bird," he said ominously, "and if ye call me little once more I'll spike ye with my broadsword!"

Graculus said he would bear it in mind, and after some discussion Ronf allowed himself to be carried down the valley to Noggin's castle.

Because he was an ambassador, Noggin had to receive him formally in the throne room.

29

The trumpets sounded. The little man walked down the long throne room between the ranks of Nog warriors assembled there. The top of his pointed hat came no higher than their belts.

"Giants, all giants," he muttered to himself.

At the foot of the throne he stopped and spoke in a loud voice.

"Greetings, Noggin the Nog."

Noggin looked down.

"Oh there you are! Greetings, little man."

Noggin sat on the steps of the throne and heard the tale that Ronf had to tell. It was a terrible tale. Ronf told how the peaceful farmers of the Hot-water Valley were hiding in holes and caves for fear of a huge dragon that was rampaging up and down the valley trampling their crops and houses.

The little man bent his knee and bowed.

"Prince Noggin," he said. "The Hot-water Valley is part of the Land of Nog. I have travelled many days through the snow in the great forests to bring you the humble greetings of my people and their prayer that you will deliver them from this monster before they starve."

Noggin rose to his feet. He called to the Captain of the Guard, the fierce Thor Nogson.

"Thor Nogson, are you any good at fighting dragons?"

Thor Nogson was surprised at the question but he answered truly.

"I don't know, I have never tried."

"Well, make ready for an expedition. We are going to the Hot-water Valley to fight a dragon!"

Noggin and Thor Nogson took a long sledge with six strong dogs. They loaded it with provisions, sat Graculus and Ronf on the top and, as the sun rose, they left the castle and set off up the winding lanes of the hill farms.

Many hours they travelled and climbed. They reached the high snow-fields where the wind blows cold.

The warm spring days seemed far behind them as their sledge skimmed over the frozen snow towards the dark forest of Troldeskow. There were no paths in the forest of Troldeskow because it had been planted in the days of magic by a black sorcerer who gave the trees the power to move about when nobody was watching.

The Nogs halted at the edge of the forest. "That is the only way," said Ronf. "Whatever perils there may be, our way lies through the forest."

"Well in that case I suppose we shall have to go that way," said Noggin, "but I don't like the idea, I am sure we shall get lost."

"I will fly above you," said Graculus. "I can fly above the trees to show you the way."

And so, into the dark silent forest they
went. There was no path and they knew
they were leaving no trail behind them
and they would never find the way back
again because the trees would have
moved to hide their tracks. Often, Noggin felt
sure they were lost, but each time he looked up
he saw Graculus circling in the sky above them.

  Then, as the light began to fade, at last the trees
thinned out. The ground grew steep, they came up out
of the forest and saw before them the vast shining walls of
the Glass Mountains glinting in the evening sun.

  They made camp and a fire of pinewood. They had boiled eggs
for tea with toast to dip in them and everybody was glad they had
come so far without mishap.

All, that is, save Graculus, who looked sad and puzzled. "I know this place," he said. "I was never here before and yet I know it well."

"Perhaps you dreamed it, Graculus," said Noggin.

"Dreamed it? Perhaps I did, but I know that if I fly over there to the right of the sun I shall see a lake of salt water among tall green trees." Graculus craned his neck as if to see over the mountain. "There are fish in the lake," he added. "Blue fish, good to eat."

Noggin though for a moment. "Where were you born, Graculus?" he asked.

"I do not know," said the bird. "A trader gave my egg to Nooka's mother. She set me by the stove to hatch and raised me from a chick, but where I came from, or in what nest my egg was laid, nobody knows."

"Go now, Graculus, while it is still light," said Noggin the Nog. "Go now and find the green trees around a lake, for it may be your egg remembers what it never saw and there you will find your home."

Without another word Graculus lifted himself from the ground and flew away. Soon Noggin, Thor Nogson, Ronf and six tired dogs slept around the dying fire.

In the morning the Nogs made a hut, gave the dogs plenty of food and told them to guard the sledge. Then they took their climbing ropes and followed Ronf up the steep track over the Glass Mountains.

It was a hard steep climb to the ledge where the tunnel led through the mountain wall. It was the only way through. Ronf cursed, shouted and pulled at the Nogs, but the tunnel was too narrow, they could not go through. They made their way back to the ledge.

"Look! There's Graculus!" shouted Thor Nogson. They waved their arms and a green bird swooped down and landed beside them.

"AAAARK," he said.

"What do you mean Aark?" said Noggin angrily. "We can't get through the tunnel."

"AAAARK," said the bird, looking up into the sky. Slowly, like leaves, a dozen green birds glided down and perched around them. Then Graculus himself arrived and told them his glad news. He had found the lake just as he had dreamed, but what he had not seen in his dream was that the grove of green trees was the home of his ancestors, the home of the great green birds.

Graculus and his family made a harness of the climbing ropes, and as easily as if they were twigs they lifted the Nogs over the top of the Glass Mountain and laid them gently on the fertile ground of the Hot-water Valley, a strange rich, steamy place in this world of ice and snow.

Ronf was crouching in a trench.

"Quick! In here! It's coming, I can hear its footsteps," he whispered. They crouched still in the trench and listened.

The heavy footsteps came closer, the ground shook. Noggin caught a glimpse of a huge frosty head which passed over them. The footsteps died away. They came out of their hiding place.

"Where does it live?" asked Noggin.

"Up there, look!" said Ronf.

They watched the dragon, huge even in the distance, fly heavily down into a high valley in the mountain wall.

"Come on, Thor Nogson," said Noggin, "we will walk."

It was a long walk. They passed the tiny houses of the little people, and everywhere they saw the dragon's footprints and nowhere did they see a living person.

Soon they reached the hills and began to climb. They climbed to the high valley over rocks and ice and up a steep little hill of scales.

"That's odd," said Noggin, "I wonder where it can be. It was here just now."

It was there, they were standing on it.

The dragon felt the small creatures on its back and cried out with delight.

"People!" it cried. "People!"

Its breath blew on the Nogs and in an instant they were frozen to a block of frost, for this was an Ice Dragon and its breath was cold.

"Oh dear!" it wailed. "I've done it again!"

Very gently it picked up the Nogs and flew down the valley to the geysers, the steaming hot water spouts that gave the valley its name. There, slowly, the Nogs thawed out and shivered.

"Oh I must be more careful!" cried the dragon. "I really must! It is so long since I spoke to anybody I had forgotten about the ice. Oh I am glad to see you. Do you know, I have been searching this valley for three weeks and I haven't seen a soul? It has been most extraordinary, just as if

38

people had been hiding from me! I do hope they haven't! I should be most upset to think of people hiding from me. It's not as if I was an angry dragon, it's just that I want to go back to bed and I can't. I haven't been to bed for three weeks and I do feel tired. Imagine not going to bed for three weeks, I do wish I could go to bed again, I really do."

The dragon stopped talking, wiped away a tear and started talking again.

"Oh dear, here I am chatting away about my own troubles and we aren't even introduced. I am Grolliffe, just an ordinary small Ice Dragon, established clerical grade. My home is - or was - that cave in the high hills. A lovely cold cave it was, and then suddenly, a few weeks ago it became hot. Yes, hot and full of smoke. I had to come out! I had to! Ice Dragons, you know, can't take heat and smoke! We melt!"

The dragon was flapping its wings with excitement. The cold wind from them made Noggin and Thor Nogson cling together for warmth.

"I've tried to go back dozens of times," wailed the dragon. "Dozens of times, but the cave's always full of smoke. I daren't go in and I do want to go back to bed. I do! I want to go back to bed! I do!"

Sadness overcame the huge beast. It gave a sob like a small clap of thunder and laid its head on the ground. A tear fell from its eye.

Noggin approached and patted the cold scaly head.

"Now, do not worry too much, Grolliffe," he said. "I am Noggin the Nog. I have come here specially to … er … well … put things in order. Show us your cave."

The dragon cheered up at once and hoisted the Nogs swiftly up to the high valley where they saw the mouth of a cave between the rocks.

"See!" it cried. "Smoke!"

A small plume of smoke was rising from the cave mouth. Noggin and Thor Nogson peered into the smoky darkness. They could see nothing.

"We must go in and look," said Noggin.

Thor Nogson, Captain of the Royal Guard was a brave man. He said, "I will go in there, I'm not afraid."

He drew his sword and crept down over the rocks to the cave mouth. Silently he made his way down the long passage until, as his eyes grew used to the dimness, he saw a high chamber lit by the faint flickering glow of a bonfire.

Two more things he saw and both of them filled him with amazement. One was the vast glittering heap of jewels, precious stones, silver and gold ornaments and weapons that covered the floor. The other was the tall angular evil figure of Noggin's uncle, Nogbad the Bad, who was shovelling the stuff into sacks and chuckling to himself.

"Huh, huh, huh. Riches beyond the dreams of avarice! Jewels for the ransom of a hundred emperors! Huh, huh, huh ..."

Thor Nogson backed away out of the cave.

"There's your uncle Nogbad in there!"

"Nogbad!"

"Yes and there's treasure, jewels and stuff. Masses of it. He's bagging it up in sacks."

"Oh no!" wailed the dragon. "It isn't mine! No he mustn't! I shall lose my position and it's so hard for a small Ice Dragon to get work nowadays. But worse than that, the treasure belongs to the Dragons' Friendly Society. I am the Hon. Treasurer you know, and if any of it is stolen the dragons will know, and from the fiery caves, grottoes and volcanoes they will rampage. Yes, rampage and beleaguer and wreak! They will breathe fire and vengeance over all the lands of Mankind until they have collected a new treasure just as rich as the old. It will really be most inconvenient for everybody!"

"Huh, huh, huh!"
Nogbad was standing in the cave mouth.
"I say, Nogbad," called Noggin. "I say, I would like a word with you!"
"Come on in, Noggin," said Nogbad in a friendly voice. He stepped back into the cave. Noggin was halfway to the cave mouth when the cannon went off.

The blast blew him over backwards.

"Huh, huh, huh," chuckled Nogbad, standing by a golden cannon from the dragons' treasure. "That time I only loaded it with gunpowder. Next time I shall load it with diamonds and rubies and they will cut you to shrebbons!"

"But Nogbad, listen!" cried Noggin, wiping the soot from his eyes. "That treasure belongs to the Dragons' Friendly Society and if you steal it the dragons will …"

"A fig for your Friendly Society," sneered Nogbad. "There's riches here beyond all my dreams and it's mine! Mine! All mine! Tell your lazy old dragon to come and get it if he wants it. The cannon is waiting!"

"Psst, Noggin," came a whisper from behind a rock. Ronf was there keeping out of sight of the dragon.

"Oh there you are, Ronf," said Noggin. "Come and meet Grolliffe."

Ronf did not like this suggestion, but Noggin picked him up, carried him over to the dragon and introduced him.

Grolliffe looked at the tiny frightened man.

"Oh isn't he small! I had no idea they were so small!"

That was enough for Ronf. His fear forgotten, he leaped to his feet and waved his sword under the dragon's nose.

"I'm not small! I'm the biggest in the valley! I'm just not a giant like these Nogs."

The dragon backed away mumbling apologies. They settled down to wait for Nogbad.

"Dragon," said Ronf. "Do you block up the mouth of the cave when you are in there?"

"Oh yes," said the dragon. "I make a point of it, I lie right across it."

"Then in that case," went on Ronf, "this Nogbad must have got in some other way and if so he has probably got out again the same way."

Ronf was right. Grolliffe flew over to a ledge above the cave mouth and blew on the cannon until it glazed over with ice. They entered the cave.

"Some of it is gone!" wailed the dragon. "Oh what shall we do?"

"Find the other way out and catch Nogbad," said Noggin.

Thor Nogson found it. He stepped on a jewelled cloak and fell through it down a narrow dug-out passage. Noggin and Ronf followed.

Here were more caves and tunnels, but Nogbad's way was marked by a trail of spilt jewels. It led to a cave on the outside of the mountain wall.

"This is where we left the dogs!" cried Noggin. "Where are they?"

The hut was there, but the sledge and the dogs were gone.

"Look over there!" shouted Thor Nogson. In the distance they saw a tiny black sledge speeding over the snow up the pass towards Lapland. Around it a cloud of green birds was circling and swooping and diving to harass its way.

Then, with a roar like the wind of a winter storm, the gentle dragon, angry at last, shot out from the mountain wall.

"After him, ye horny lizard!" cried Ronf. The dragon's leather wings beat the sky as it hurtled away. It turned in the air above the distant sledge and dived in a trail of cold mist to blow one long breath on the speeding villain.

One breath was enough. The sledge with its load of jewels and Nogbad froze fast to the snow in a glittering lump.

That evening a wet, weary Nogbad carried the last of the treasure back into the dragon's cave. He signed his name to a piece of dragon paper on which was written his promise never to steal again and then he slunk away into the forest.

The dragon made a speech.

"Noggin the Nog," it said. "The Dragons' Friendly Society thanks you. On their behalf I take pleasure in presenting you with this gong. If ever you are in danger, beat it with silver and cry, 'Come dragons! Come dragons!' and believe me, dragons will come to your aid. I am sure you will find it useful. Only …" the dragon yawned. "Not too often, most of us are old and retired nowadays, and I for one would be glad of another thousand years' sleep."

The dragon settled down comfortably on its pile of jewels.

"Sleep well Grolliffe," said Noggin the Nog. "Sleep for a thousand years."

The Nogs rolled a stone across the mouth of the cave as Ronf and the little people of the Hot-water Valley sang a lullaby.

Oh lully, lully, oh lully my monster,
Sleep my scaly friend
And fold your horny claws and slumber,
Happy in the end.

3

The FLYING MACHINE

N THE LANDS OF THE NORTH, WHERE THE BLACK
rocks stand guard against the cold sea, in the dark
night that is very long, the men of the Northlands sit
by their great log fires and they tell a tale. They tell
of Noggin, Prince of the Nogs, who sailed beyond the black
ice at the edge of the world to fetch Nooka, Princess of the
Nooks, to be his Queen. They tell of the magic gong or
medal which was given to Noggin by Grolliffe, the ice
dragon, who guarded the dragons' treasure in the Hot-water
Valley. This medal was magic. If it was beaten with silver it
would call dragons to your aid.

Noggin had no need of the aid of dragons. He and his
queen lived in peace and happiness in the little town beside
the harbour.

Summers and winters came and went and all were content; all save one. Peace and happiness were boring for the fierce Thor Nogson, the captain of the King's Guard. He stood on the harbour wall and gazed out to sea, dreaming of the old days when there were battles and warriors and brave deeds in the land of Nog.

Noggin came and spoke to him. He said: "How would you like to sail a great ship, Thor Nogson? How would you like to sail a great ship high in the clouds, over the mountains and over the sea to far strange lands?"

Thor Nogson grunted crossly. "Of course I would like to, but I am not a bird and I am not a magician."

"No," said Noggin. "I already have a bird in my service and I have no need of a magician. I have an inventor. Come and see what Olaf the Lofty and Graculus have made."

Down beside the harbour, Graculus, the green bird, and Olaf the Lofty were arguing furiously.

"Feathers!" shouted Graculus.

"Leather!" shouted Olaf.

"Quiet!" shouted Noggin. "Is the machine finished yet? I want to show it to Thor Nogson!"

"All but the wing coverings," said Olaf. "We shall use leather."

"Feathers!" muttered Graculus.

"There, Thor Nogson," said Noggin. "What do you think of that?"

"It's a boat," said Thor Nogson. "It looks quite a good little boat, but what is the funny shaped mast for? And all those rods and levers and bits of wood and that machine in the middle? Where does the sail go?"

"Ah, I will tell you," began Olaf the Lofty. "Years ago, when I was a boy

my father, who was, as you know, something of a magician and descended from Long Olaf, the sorcerer of Nudrug ... Well, he ..."

"It is a flying machine, I invented it myself," said Graculus.

"*You* invented it!" Olaf went scarlet with rage.

"Yes, it is driven by clockwork. That machine in the middle is ... eeerkmm ..." Olaf the Lofty had grabbed Graculus's beak and gripped it shut.

"As I was saying ... this flying machine is driven by clockwork. You turn that handle which winds up the great spring, and that in its turn drives the wings which are pivoted to the mast and are covered in leather."

"Feathers!" shouted Graculus, breaking free.

"Leather!" shouted Olaf.

"Quiet!" shouted Noggin. "No more squabbling. Olaf, you had better go and get leather for the wings. It is easier to get than feathers and I want this machine finished quickly. Thor Nogson is waiting to fly in it."

"Fly?" exclaimed Thor Nogson aghast.

"Yes, you always say you want excitement?"

"Yes, but ... well ... oh."

Graculus was looking down into the water of the harbour.

"Hi! What is this thing floating in the harbour? It looks like a jar or something."

It was a jar. When they hauled it out with a crane, Olaf gripped his toes and shuddered.

"Bad magic," he said. "It makes my toes tingle. It smells of sorcery! It smells of bad magic."

"It smells of bad seaweed to me," said Graculus.

"Well, put it in the royal armoury for the moment and get on with finishing the boat," said Noggin the Nog.

They wheeled the jar to the royal armoury and set it down on the stone floor.

Late that night, the door opened stealthily and a glint of candlelight showed through the crack.

"Put out that light, Olaf," whispered Thor Nogson. "I can hear voices."

The voices came, it seemed, from inside the jar itself.

"Is all quiet in this place, oh gentle jar, oh pitcher?" came one voice.

"All is quiet, oh master, I hear no sound," replied another.

"So here is my journey's end and yours, my prison cell."

From inside the jar came the sound of sharp tapping.

"Have mercy, master! Spare my brittle skin!" came a plaintive cry.

"Enough of words, vile gourd! Your time is up!"

CRASH!

The jar fell in shards to the stone floor and there stood a dark man carrying a bundle. He looked around.

"Ah, so this is the hall of the barbarians! We have done well. Now we must move fast. The throne room will be above ... and in the glass case ..." The man ran swiftly up the stone stairs. Thor Nogson followed quietly.

"Ah yes," said the man. "A truly elegant bauble, but let us not be too sudden. Are we observed? ... Yes, a helmet I see."

Thor Nogson was hiding behind a high seat. The man ran across and tapped his helmet.

"Come fellow," he said. "It is written that the path of the bringer of glad tidings shall be strewn with the petals of roses."

"Oh, is it?" grunted Thor Nogson. "What are you doing here?"

"Is your master called Noggin, oh cow-hatted one? Do they call him Prince of the Nogs?"

"They do."

"Well lead me to him, barbarian, and all shall be made clear as the light that shines in the garden of …"

"I am already here," said Noggin.

"Is it even so?" The man bowed low. "Oh Royal Nog, from my master Emir Ahmed el Ahmed, ruler of the land of Silver Sand, I bring you greetings, greetings and this unworthy trifle, this poor gift from his royal collection, this silken carpet of strange design."

He unrolled a small beautiful carpet on the floor before the throne.

"Oh my toes! My toes!" cried Olaf the Lofty, and he fled from the hall. The man sat cross-legged on the carpet and Noggin ordered the guards to bring him food and drink.

"Welcome to our humble palace," said Noggin. "I am afraid we have nothing to show you as handsome as that carpet you brought."

"Ah, but you have," said the man. "I see a crown in that glass case. Is it the crown of the Northlands?"

"It is," said Noggin. "I wear it for state occasions you know. Thor Nogson, get it out and show it to our guest."

Thor Nogson took out the crown and handed it to their guest.

"Thanks indeed, oh cow-hatted one. It is indeed an elegant bauble. Quite exquisite."

Olaf the Lofty came back into the hall. He was wearing his grandfather's ring, which was a guard against magic and stopped his toes tingling. He sat down.

"Ah good," said the man. "I will tell you a story concerning this crown. To the court of my master, Ahmed el Ahmed, there came a while ago a tall barbarian who claims that he is the rightful King of the Northlands.

He claims that his crown was stolen by a wicked nephew and a green bird and ... No!"

Thor Nogson's hand froze to his sword-hilt as a spark of magic flashed from the man's fingers.

"No! You cannot draw your sword, cow-hatted barbarian! Ah, the dawn has come to tear the veil of night. See, I rise to take my leave of you." The carpet, with the man on it, rose slowly into the air.

"I take the crown, barbarians, and none of you can move until I am gone." Olaf, protected by his ring, leapt to his feet.

"Away!" shouted the man, and the carpet tilted and flew to the window.

Olaf grabbed it and was dragged across the floor, out of the window and away. Once they were out of sight, the magic spell was broken and the Nogs ran to the window. Olaf, unhurt, was in a tree. The magic carpet was gone.

"I've got his shoe!" shouted Olaf the Lofty. "Go after him in the flying machine!"

Graculus collected the shoe from Olaf and flew with it to the harbour where Noggin and Thor Nogson boarded the flying machine and cast off.

"Wind the handle, Thor Nogson!" ordered Noggin.

Thor Nogson was terrified, but he wound the handle. Noggin pulled the starting lever and the flying machine lurched forwards. Its great leather wings rose and flapped the air. The machine lurched and hopped as the wings beat faster. Suddenly they rose from the sea and the wings were carrying them aloft. They were flying.

Far ahead in the distance they saw the magic carpet speeding away from them.

"We are gaining on him!" shouted Graculus.

The man on the magic carpet turned his head.

"So! We are hunted. The magic carpet is slow compared to the flying machine, but perhaps a little cleverer. Now, a pinch of snuff perhaps."

From his silken garments the man took a tiny silver snuff-box.

"Would you care for a pinch of snuff, Noggin?" he asked the empty air.

He threw a pinch of snuff over his shoulder and it became a thick black storm-cloud across the sky.

"Fly through that, cow-hatted fools," he laughed, but the thunder drowned his laughter.

The storm caught the flying machine and tossed it through the swirling black clouds. The leather wings tore and it fell like a dead leaf to the sea below. The flying carpet flew on.

That night, Thor Nogson, Graculus and Noggin slept under a canvas sheet in their boat, which was drifting calmly on the sea. They had no oars and there was no wind to fill a sail.

Suddenly Thor Nogson sat up.

"Listen!" he whispered.

They heard a deep-throated clucking sound.

They peered out from under their canvas. Their boat was floating in a small bay which was lined with palm trees. The moon was shining on the sea. The only sound was the rippling of tiny waves and these occasional deep-throated clucking sounds. Graculus flew to the top of the mast, looked round once and flew straight down again.

"Great Orps," he whispered. "Keep quiet!"

"What are Great Orps?" asked Noggin.

"Birds," said Graculus, "very large birds. They are settling down for the night. When the moon sets they will sleep. We must wait."

They waited. When the moon had set and the birds had stopped grunting, the Nogs took ropes and crept out among the trees. They saw the enormous bodies of the sleeping birds perched in the trees and they very gently tied ropes to their tail feathers.

As the grey light of dawn lit the rim of the sea, the Nogs took shields and swords and beat them together. The huge birds jerked awake. With terrible raucous howls, they flapped their great bodies into the air and flew away, leaving behind seventeen perfect tail feathers, each as long as the wing of the flying machine.

"As I said," said Graculus proudly, "feathers are best for flying machines."

With ropes and nails they fixed the huge feathers to the flying machine. Thor Nogson wound the handle and they were off.

"It works!" shouted Noggin. "It flies better than ever!"

The flying machine clicked and whirred as it flew strongly southwards towards the Land of Silver Sand.

Haroun ibn Daud was an ordinary, nice, kind, old gentleman, who lived in a white house beside a lake and palm trees in the Land of Silver Sand. His servant was a genie, a magic spirit of white smoke, which he kept in a jar.

"See, oh smoky one," said the old gentleman. "The lake and trees are beautiful but something is needed to complete the picture. A flight of perfect white swans … yes, that would do."

"Your wish is my command," replied the genie.

Something swept across the sky, turned and landed with a long splash across the lake.

"That was quick, oh smoky one," exclaimed the old gentleman, "but I ordered a flight of white swans, not a dirty great boat with feathers!" "None of my doing, oh master." "Oh well, back into your pot then." Haroun ibn Daud walked to the lake to greet his visitors. He led the dusty Nogs and their bird to his house and bade his genie offer them refreshment. Noggin told the whole story to their host who heard it with a grave face.

"This is a sad country," he said, when Noggin had finished. "The Emperor Ahmed el Ahmed is no more emperor than I am. His nephew is the true monarch but the wicked Ahmed has cast him in a dungeon. Your coming will be a great deliverance for us, for I feel you are a man of justice. It is written that the bringer of justice shall come from afar and all must help his way."

64

Haroun ibn Daud disguised the Nogs as a respectable Arab merchant and his lady and set them on camels. He handed a small jar to Noggin.

"Take my servant," he said. "If you are in danger, draw the cork and the genie will come forth to guard you!"

Noggin and Thor Nogson took leave of the kind old gentleman and pointed their camels southwards towards the distant white city.

Graculus flew on ahead and met them at the gate. He led them aside through a dark alley.

"I have been speaking to the vultures," he said. "Leave the camels here and walk to the back of the golden palace. There is a blind man there who sells sweetmeats. He will tell you a secret way into the palace if you give him a piece of silver, but you must … talk very politely like they do here!"

The Nogs walked through the dusty alleys to the back of the golden palace where they heard the plaintive cry of the blind sweetseller.

"Sweetmeats! Delights from Turkey! The eyes of bulls! Farthing bananas! Buy a sherbert dab, oh gracious masters!"

"We would buy something of greater worth, oh man of the dark," began Noggin. "Is is written that an uncle sits in his newphew's seat and the golden bird of justice has flown from the silver tower in the garden of … where was I? I've got a silver piece somewhere."

"Well, hand it over and stop talking nonsense," said the blind man. "The door is in the wall behind me. Turn the head of the peacock and it will open … Sweetmeats! All sorts of liquorice! Who'll buy my sweetmeats?"

The Nogs crept stealthily into the palace. They found themselves in a narrow passage which led to a parapet under the roof.

"Keep down!" whispered Noggin. "Look!"

They watched the flying carpet sail across the sky and float down into the courtyard of the palace.

"He took his time," said Thor Nogson.

"Come on," whispered Graculus, "in here."

They crept through another narrow passage and found themselves behind a pierced screen in a high place above the emperor's audience chamber.

They saw the messenger with only one shoe bow before his master and deliver Noggin's crown. They saw the emperor clap his hands and a door open. The figure that emerged was known to them all. It was Noggin's wicked uncle, Nogbad the Bad.

"See, barbarian," said the emperor, "I have a gift for you."

"He's going to put your crown on Nogbad's head," hissed Thor Nogson.
"Look! He mustn't do that!"

In his excitement, Thor Nogson sneezed and dropped the Arab's
slipper. It fell with a slap on the face of the emperor.

"What is this?" he cried.

"It is my shoe, oh
Master of the World,"
said the messenger, "but
I did not throw it. It fell
from above."

Guards were sent to
seize the Nogs and bring
them before the emperor.

"So, Noggin, we meet again," sneered Nogbad.

"Oh! Hallo, Nogbad! Been up to your old tricks again have you?" said Noggin.

"What me? I have not stolen anything," said Nogbad.

"Are these your friends, Nogbad?" asked the puzzled emperor.

"Not my friends," said Nogbad. "This is Noggin the Nog, who called himself King of the Northlands and wore my crown. He is my nephew."

"Ah, these nephews!" chuckled the emperor. "Such a nuisance! Shall I have them slain?"

"No, wait a minute," said Noggin.

He pulled out the cork from Haroun ibn Daud's jar. From it emerged a whitish cloud which slowly formed itself into a genie.

"What is your will, oh master?" it enquired anxiously.

"Well, do your stuff," said Noggin. "This emperor is threatening to have us slain. Turn him into a toad or something."

"So!" laughed the emperor. "You would use magic?"

He clapped his hands. One of the guards raised his sword and brought it down on a huge jar. It smashed with a noise like thunder and a black cloud many times larger than Haroun ibn Daud's genie formed in the air.

The small genie condensed rapidly into droplets and wriggled back into its jar, pausing only to grab the cork and pull it in.

The black genie lowered its toothy head and surveyed the Nogs.

"Do I eat them now or tear them limb from limb to feed the vultures?"

Noggin was whispering to Thor Nogson.

"Why do you whisper together, barbarians?" snapped the emperor.

"Oh, I gave away my last silver coin," explained Noggin. "Do you happen to have anything made of silver I could borrow for a moment?"

"Here, barbarian dog," said the emperor. "Take this, it will not save you." He threw down a silver piece.

"Thank you," said Noggin, and taking out the medal the dragon had given him he started to beat it with silver and call. "Come dragons! Come dragons!"

"Dragons!" laughed the emperor. "Dragons indeed! My genie eats dragons for breakfast."

"Come dragons! Come dragons!"

"My genie picks them up, fiery breath and all and swallows them with one gulp. He ..."

The emperor stopped speaking as he felt the palace begin to shake under the heavy footsteps of the ice dragon.

"Oh Noggin, Noggin, what a terribly hot place!" wailed the ice dragon as its great scaly head appeared in the arched doorway. "Oh, and what nasty looking friends you have!"

"What is this lizard?" roared the genie. "I guard the emperor Ahmed el Ahmed, Master of the World, and I will bite you in pieces!"

"Oh! Isn't he rude!"
cried the ice dragon. "Come
outside, you lump of hot air, and I will
blow you away!"

 The genie formed in the sky like a huge
storm-cloud and prepared to devour the fiery dragon, but Grolliffe was
an *ice* dragon which was not what the genie expected. Grolliffe blew
round and through and over the great toothy smog, and his icy breath
turned it until it spun like a ball and shrank away to an ice cube.

 The emperor and Nogbad lost no time.
They jumped on to the magic carpet
and made off. Graculus just had time
to dive down on Nogbad and snatch
the crown before the magic carpet
headed Northwards away from that
troubled land.

 "I must go now," said the ice dragon. "It
has been nice seeing you again, Noggin, Thor Nogson, Graculus, and I
was glad to help, but I must not stay in this hot place another minute or I
shall melt away! Don't worry about those two on the magic carpet. I will
pick them up on the way home and they can spend a few years cooling
off and counting my jewels."

So the ice dragon flew away and that is nearly the end of the story.

The emperor's guards rejoiced that their cruel master had fled and straight away they brought the young king from the dungeons. Haroun ibn Daud brought the flying machine on a carriage drawn by six white camels.

The Nogs took leave of the young king and the old magician. Thor Nogson wound the handle and, laden with jewels and gifts, the flying machine lifted itself from the calm water of the harbour and turned Northwards on the long journey home.

4

The OMRUDS

IN THE LANDS OF THE NORTH, WHERE THE BLACK
rocks stand guard against the cold sea, in the dark
night that is very long, the men of the Northlands
sit by their great log fires and they tell a tale. They
tell of Noggin, Prince of the Nogs, and how the King-under-
the-Hill helped him to defeat the great crows, and how Noggin
made him a garden of flowers and trees.

One fine day in Summer, Noggin the Nog and his friend Olaf the Lofty,
the court inventor, were walking on the hills behind the town.

"Come Olaf," said Noggin. "How can you look so sad when the world
is so pleasant?"

"Ah, Noggin," said Olaf miserably, "I am sad. My days as court inventor
are numbered. Look down there at your castle, your town and harbour."

Noggin looked at them and the sight pleased him. Olaf shook his head sadly.

"See," he said. "The perfect city. The culture of the Nogs has reached its peak. I have been inventing things all my life and now I know that there is nothing left to invent! It has been a good life, but it must end ... ah well."

Olaf wiped away a tear and Noggin roared with laughter. Under their feet the earth shook.

"An earthquake!" cried Olaf.

The rumbling increased and suddenly the top of the hill behind them cracked open. Out shot steam and rock and a tiny, skinny man in a tunic.

"It works! It works!" he cried. "It works! Oh, my eyes! My eyes! Oh, the light! It hurts!" The tiny man clapped his hands over his eyes to protect them from the light as he rolled over and over down the hill towards the stream.

"The waterfall!" shouted Noggin. "He'll fall in the stream and go over the waterfall!"

Olaf lifted his tunic and capered away down the hill. He threw himself on to an overhanging branch and grasped the man's skinny leg as the rushing water swept him by. The Nogs carried the cold unconscious person into a cave and made a fire of twigs.

In the warm, dark place, the man stirred and coughed and sat up.

"Oh, ugh, oh, what happened?" he said in a small thin voice. "Ah yes, I remember! It exploded … but it worked, it worked!"

The little man jumped with joy. "Oh, excuse me!" he said. "I must introduce myself. My name is Groont. I am an Omrud. I am court inventor to the King-under-the-Hill. I have just invented an invention that will change the course of History and bring a golden age of leisure and happiness to all mankind!"

"Well, my name is Noggin the Nog," said Noggin, "and this is Olaf the Lofty, my court inventor. He has just saved you from being swept over the waterfall."

The Omrud bowed low.

"Greetings, Noggin the Nog. We have heard many tales of your adventures even in our deep place under the hill. And to you, Olaf the Lofty, I owe my life. If ever you need anything an Omrud can give, name it and it shall be yours. Nogs, I thank you."

The Omrud bowed again, turned and walked away into the cave. The Nogs heard a door creak and slam, then silence.
The Omrud had gone back under the hill.

Olaf was puzzled. He was puzzled and worried and extremely annoyed. The Omrud obviously thought he had invented something new and important. But what could he possibly have invented that Olaf himself hadn't thought of already? Olaf was sure there was nothing left to invent. Had he not told Noggin so?

As he sat worrying in his little room, Olaf heard a soft clunk-clunking noise outside, and heard a faint tap-tap on his door. Olaf opened the door.

"Oh! Somebody has left a green glass jar on my doorstep," said he.

As he said it the glass jar lifted itself on little feet and ambled into Olaf's room. There it tipped over on its side and out crawled Groont the Omrud.

"Green glass!" he said proudly. "My own invention. We use it when we go outside. The light hurts our eyes you know. Olaf, the King-under-the-Hill greets you and thanks you for saving my life. He says that as a reward you are to have the secret of my invention. Here it is."

He gave Olaf a piece of parchment with a picture and some writing on it. Olaf read the writing:

The mountain stream runs swiftly;
Hold it fast in iron.
The fire burns like the sun;
Keep it close.
The mist rises and blows away;
Catch it. It is your servant.

"Yes," said Groont. "You can use copper if you like, but it's not so strong as iron."

"Oh er, yes … yes, of course," said Olaf, thoroughly confused. "Yes, iron I think, iron every time … yes."

Groont, his work done, bowed to Olaf, climbed into his jar, tipped himself upright and ambled out of the door.

Olaf was still standing looking at the paper.

"Oh dear. It doesn't even make sense," he muttered.

He read it many times and puzzled and puzzled over the picture until slowly an idea came to him. He jumped up and ran about the palace collecting old iron and brassware and odds and ends.

Far into the night he hammered and banged and muttered to himself as the city of the Nogs slept under the stars.

The next morning, Noggin and Graculus were standing on the path in front of the castle walls, looking at the boats in the harbour, when a rumbling crash like a clap of thunder was heard and a section of the castle burst open. Out shot steam and stones and a large skinny man in a tunic. It was Olaf the Lofty.

"It works!" he shouted. "It works! It works! My invention works!"

"*Your* invention, Olaf?" asked Noggin.

"Well, er … yes … No … Partly mine anyway," said Olaf.

Noggin was very uncertain about the value of such a noisy invention, but Olaf was sure it was important and he spent the next two weeks in a frenzy of excitement, making up a special machine which was to pull Noggin's golden carriage on his Birthday Drive.

The day of the Birthday Drive came and Olaf stood beside his invention which was tied to the shafts of the golden carriage.

"My fire machine," he said proudly.

Thor Nogson sat on the driver's seat of the carriage and drew his sword.

Noggin and Nooka sat in the carriage.

The people cheered and Olaf climbed on to his machine. It gave a shriek like a trodden cat and lurched forward. The carriage jolted forward after it and slowly, with huge puffs and steamy clanks, the fire machine hauled the carriage towards the town hall and Noggin's Birthday Banquet.

"Going very well!" shouted Olaf to Thor Nogson, whose eyes were full of cinders.

Olaf opened another tap, pulled a lever and the fire machine, which had been trundling, began to go faster. It went at a canter and then a gallop. Then it began to race along, capering and lurching wildly.

Olaf wrestled with the controls, but the lever was stuck.

They passed he town hall and the astonished elders at a tremendous pace.

Thor Nogson, clinging to the carriage, decided that it was time for him to defend his king against the monstrous machine and he slashed through the rope.

Olaf on his fire machine went on alone. Faster and faster it went, puffing and bounding and clanking up the hill towards the high cliff.

Graculus, seeing the danger, flew down and gripped Olaf by the scruff of the neck. Olaf tried to push him away but Graculus managed to drag him off the machine.

Olaf sat on the ground and watched his fire machine thunder to the peak of the cliff and leap off the edge.

It sailed in an arc of fire and steam to the still water of the fjord far below. With a splash and a great hissing cloud of steam, it was gone for ever.

Olaf wept, but three upturned glass jars lurking in a cavemouth nearby were laughing and laughing.

"Omruds!" shouted Olaf, scarlet with rage. "It's their fault! Wait till I catch them!"

The Omruds fled into the cave with Olaf in close pursuit. By the time Noggin and Thor Nogson arrived he was gone. He had vanished into the cave.

"Olaf will be all right," said Noggin. "The Omruds will not hurt him. Come on everybody. It is time for my Birthday Banquet. Olaf will come home when it suits him."

Olaf did not come home that day, or the next. In the end, Noggin and Thor Nogson went to the cave and tried to follow Olaf's path. They must have been expected because an Omrud with a torch appeared and led them to the hall of the King-under-the-Hill.

The old king greeted Noggin with great pleasure and ceremony. They took tea together and the king explained the history of the Omruds and how they had been driven from their caves in Nudrug by a tall man who had come from the North beyond the Glass Mountains.

"He was a giant like you Nogs," said the king, "but he was unpleasant and his friends were black crows. He wanted the caves, so his crows just drove us out. Since then we have lived inside the hill, and now the light of day hurts our eyes, but in those days at Nudrug we had meadows and fields which we could call our own. But I am boring you with our troubles. You came to find your angry Olaf. He is in our laboratories with Groont. He is very happy. They are working on a diminishing fluid."

"A diminishing fluid?" said Noggin.

"Yes, come and see."

The King-under-the-Hill led them into a laboratory where Olaf
demonstrated his diminishing fluid.

"You see this cabbage. Well, if I pour a few drops of this fluid on the
cabbage it will still be a cabbage, but it will be half
the size. Watch!"

Olaf poured a few drops on the cabbage.

Wheep!

The cabbage grew to twice the size.

"Oh dear, that shouldn't happen," said
Olaf. "I had better try again."

He tried again and ...

Wheep!

The cabbage was vast. It practically filled the cave.

"Stop!" shouted the King-under-the-Hill. "We have no use for monster cabbages!" Noggin and Thor Nogson led the disappointed Olaf away. By the time they reached the open air, Olaf was feeling less disappointed, and by the time they had reached the castle he was feeling very pleased with himself. Graculus met them and Olaf insisted on demonstrating his marvellous fluid which made things grow to twice their size. He poured a few drops on a potato plant.

Wheep!

It grew to a small tree.

"What a dangerous invention," said Graculus. "Imagine what would happen if the rats were sprinkled with it! Rats as big as wolves! In the wrong hands that could be the most dangerous stuff ever invented."

Olaf held his bottle aloft with a dramatic gesture.

"Well, in my hands it is going to be the greatest invention in the world. I shall keep it safe and use it for the benefit of all mankind!"

A large black crow glided down and neatly lifted the bottle from Olaf's hand. If flew away.

For a moment the Nogs were too amazed to move. Graculus was the first to speak.

"Well that's that," he said, "and I reckon you're well rid of it!"

"Don't be silly!" cried Noggin. "That is one of the crows of Nudrug I expect! Quick! Fly after it!"

Graculus flew. Noggin was right. The crow was flying strongly northwards towards Nudrug. Graculus flew fast but the crow had a good lead. Graculus was close behind the crow when it turned and dived into one of the caves of Nudrug. Graculus followed and in the dark of the cave he did not see who was waiting for him until a horny hand caught him by the throat and a voice he recognised greeted him.

"So Graculus, you ugly fowl, we meet again!"

"Nogbad!"

"Yes, Graculus, me! Banished, scorned, imprisoned and deprived, Nogbad still comes back to claim his rightful crown. The crown of the Northlands. And you Graculus, are going to help."

"Never!"

"Yes! You are going to tell me what is
in this little bottle that my little friend
has brought me … Tell me!"
  Nogbad shook Graculus by the throat.
  "Flying juice," croaked Graculus.
  "Flying juice?"
  "Yes, hold it close or it will fly away!"
  For a second Nogbad loosened his grip on
Graculus to hold the bottle close. That second was enough. In a cloud
of pecking, squawking crows, Graculus was away. His strong wings
lifted him out of the cave and the crows dropped behind him.
  So Graculus escaped from the clutches of the wicked Nogbad and flew
home. He told Noggin what had happened. The Nogs were sad to hear
that Nogbad the Bad was still seeking vengeance, and that he had
captured Olaf's invention. They prepared a expedition to the caves of
Nudrug. They would take their flying machine. They were carrying
provisions down to the harbour when the first of the giant crows arrived.

It flew heavily down from the sky and perched on the roof of the castle. Others came and perched beside it. Thor Nogson rallied the Royal guard. They drew their swords and marched towards the castle. Even as they approached the castle gate one of the birds pulled out the bolt and the iron gate dropped. They were locked out of the castle and Nooka was inside! Graculus flew up with a rope and pulley and fought off the birds while Noggin lowered Nooka down from her room in a basket. She was safe, but the crows still held the castle and more crows were arriving every minute. The last crow was carrying something. It was carrying a tall man in a helmet. It lowered the man gently on to the top of the gatehouse.

"Welcome me, Nogs!" cried Nogbad. "Let me hear your cheers! For I have come to set you free!"

The assembled townspeople did not cheer.

"Ugh! You are a rabble without sense," snarled Nogbad. "See my birds! Will they not tear the roofs off your houses? Will they not pluck the trees from your orchards to make their nests? Do you make me your enemy for I am your friend. I bring you a gift. I bring you freedom from the tyranny and slavery of Noggin the Nog. That is my gift!"

"Here is a gift for you, Nogbad!" came a voice from the crowd.

A large yellow thing sailed through the air and hit Nogbad's face with a splash. It was a custard pie.

"So!" snarled Nogbad. "You would defy me. Well you shall know my vengeance! ... Birds!"

Thor Nogson walked forward and stood before the gate.

"Nogbad!" he shouted. "I defy you. I challenge you to sword and shield. To fight in single combat here before my king. Nogbad, I call you a liar."

"You are a servant," sneered Nogbad. "I will not bother with you."

"Nogbad, I call you a liar and a cheat!" roared Thor Nogson.

"People of the town, listen to me ..." began Nogbad.

"Fight him! Fight Thor Nogson!" shouted the people.

"Nogbad, I call you a coward, a cringing coward!" laughed Thor Nogson.

A crafty look came over Nogbad's face. "All right, little Thor Nogson," he smiled. "I will fight you. Bird! Set me down in the place below!"

A great crow lifted him and set him down.

"So, little Thor Nogson. You would fight me!"

"I am as big as you," said Thor Nogson.

"You were," laughed Nogbad and he held the bottle over his head. He poured out a few drops and, like the cabbage, he grew to twice his normal size. Thor Nogson turned and walked away.

"So you are a coward, Thor Nogson," sneered Nogbad.

"No, you are the coward," said Noggin. "You were afraid to meet him in fair fight."

Nogbad laughed. "Well, somebody must fight me," he said. "I have taken the challenge to single combat. Somebody must fight me or I win the crown without a fight. Who will fight me?"

Nobody answered.

90

"Is it as easy as that?" smiled Nogbad. "Are you all cowards?"

On the ground before him a paving-stone shifted and tipped. A tiny figure wearing dark glasses rose from under it. He was carrying what looked like a fly-spray.

"I will fight you," said the Omrud, "I will meet you in single combat and I will beat you!"

"What is this maggot?" asked Nogbad.

"My name is Groont. I serve the King-under-the-Hill. You are Nogbad the Bad and I call you a liar, a coward and a cheat."

"I will tread on you then … there!"

Nogbad stamped forward but Groont skipped out of his way and squirted Nogbad from the other side with his fly-spray.

"Come on then, Nogbad," he taunted.

Nogbad turned and caught the spray full in his face. It did not hurt him, but his foot missed the laughing Omrud.

"Over here, Nogbad," shouted Groont and Nogbad met another burst of spray.

"What's that stuff?" he shouted
finding himself suddenly face to face
with the Omrud.

"Shrinking fluid," said the Omrud.
"Take up your sword and fight a
fair fight."

To fight a fair fight was not in
Nogbad's nature.

"Birds!" he cried "Birds! Come down and take this worm!"

Then the battle began. The Nogs with axes and swords advanced to
defend Groont from the birds, while Groont smote Nogbad smartly on
the helmet and dragged him under the paving stone to the other
Omrud's waiting below.

The crows were cowards. Without Nogbad they did not bother to fight.
Graculus had fetched some of his cousins to help and they carried
Omruds with fly-sprays of diminishing fluid who sprayed the crows until
they were smaller than starlings.

Later, the King-under-the-Hill came to feast with Noggin and brought him a present. This present was a tiny Nogbad in a cage.

"Just like a real one," exclaimed Nooka.

"It is the real one," explained the King-under-the-Hill. "We have just made him a more useful size."

Unfortunately, the size was more useful to Nogbad than they thought, because while nobody was looking he managed to reach out and tip some more shrinking fluid on himself. He became small enough to squeeze through the bars of his cage and slip away.

Nogbad stood on the window-sill with his little crows.

"Goodbye, Noggin," he said. "We shall meet again!"

Before anybody could reach him, his crows lifted the tiny figure and flew away northwards towards Nudrug.

"Let him go," said Noggin. "He is too small to do any harm. Come, Nogs, we have work to do. We have a garden to make. A garden for the King-under-the-hill."

The garden was beautiful. It had pavilions and flowers and a lake and fountains. It had a farm with cows and sheep, all, thanks to the shrinking fluid, the right size for the Omruds. And it was their own garden for ever, where they lived in peace and happiness, watched over by their friends, the giants they called the Nogs.